THIS WALKER BOOK BELONGS TO

First published 2005 by Walker Books Ltd, 87 Vauxhall Walk, London SE11 5HJ

This edition published 2006

1 2 3 4 5 6 7 8 9 10 © 2005 Caroline Glicksman

The right of Caroline Glicksman to be identified as author/illustrator of this work has been

asserted by her in accordance with the Copyright, Designs and Patents Act 1988

This book has been typeset in Albertus   Printed in China

This book is for Jessie,
who was a top dog too.

British Library Cataloguing in Publication Data: a catalogue record

for this book is available from the British Library

ISBN-13: 978-1-4063-0217-2   ISBN-10: 1-4063-0217-1

www.walkerbooks.co.uk

BIG BLACK DOG

Caroline Glicksman

WALKER BOOKS
AND SUBSIDIARIES
LONDON · BOSTON · SYDNEY · AUCKLAND

In a town far away lived

BIG BLACK DOG.

He was very ...

Whenever he went

for a walk in the park,

everyone ran away.

Big Black Dog was *so* scary that the mayor had made him **Chief Burglar-Catcher**.

But he never had anything to do. All the burglars had left town long ago because they were so afraid of him.

Emmeline's Teas & Cakes

The Barking Daily

ANOTHER CRIME-FREE MONTH

By Sniffer
Our crime correspondent

Once again, the mayor was absolutely no
that there were absolutely no
AT ALL last month in Kenn

Super-scary
The mayor said this
showed the success
of his controversial
appointment of sup
scary Big Black
Dog as Chief B
Catcher.
Read more o
and 17-25.

Only his friend Emmeline
knew Big Black Dog's secret,
which was that ...

...he was scared of

LOUD NOISES

and

spiders

and

cats

and

strawberry jelly...

...and even his
own reflection
in the mirror!

NAME Big Black Dog
POSITION Chief Burglar-Catcher

But most of all, Big Black Dog was scared
of *ever* having to catch a burglar.

Emmeline tried to help Big Black Dog to be
brave by telling him about her adventures,
but it only made him feel
more scared.

INTREPID
AVIATOR
CONQUERS
ATLANTIC
Pioneering poodle
Emmeline Yester-

Then one morning,
everyone in the town woke up
to find they had been burgled!

The mayor rang Big Black Dog.
"The whole town is counting on you
to catch the villain," he said.

Our Chief Burglar-
Catcher has the
situation under control.

Big Black Dog was

TERRIFIED.

He spent all day
hiding behind the sofa.

RING
RING

When it got dark, he decided to run away.

He wrapped a few of his favourite things
in his scarf and went to Emmeline's
tea shop to say goodbye.

But when no one answered the door,
Big Black Dog knew something was wrong.
Then he heard a muffled bark.
Emmeline was in trouble!

Closed

Big Black Dog forced the door open
and quickly rescued his friend.

"Watch out!"

gasped Emmeline.

"It's ...

BAD CAT BLING

the Burglar King!!!"

For just a second,
Big Black Dog felt all wobbly
inside. A burglar! **A cat!**

But then he felt so angry about all
the mean things the burglar had done
that he forgot he was scared and ...

OFF

Bad Cat Bling flew up in the air...

...looped the loop...

...and landed
in his very own
SWAG BAG.

Quickly, Big Black Dog phoned the mayor.
"Send round the police," he barked,
"the cat's in the bag."

"Thank you, Big Black Dog," said Emmeline.
"You were so brave!"

But Big Black Dog wasn't
feeling brave at all –
what was that loud,
scary noise outside?

Emmeline ran over
to the window.
"Look!" she said.

A huge crowd was shouting,

TOP DOG!
TOP DOG!
TOP DOG!

For the second time that day,
Big Black Dog forgot to be afraid.

No one runs away from Big Black Dog any more.
Instead, they call him Brave Black Dog
and he gets invited to lots of parties.

Sometimes he still
feels a *little* bit
scared,

FOR
BRAVERY

NAME
BRAVEBlack
Dog
POSITION
Chief
Burglar -
Catcher

but after all, he says, you can still be brave,
even if you feel like a wobbly jelly inside.

WALKER BOOKS is the world's leading
independent publisher of children's books.
Working with the best authors and illustrators
we create books for all ages, from babies
to teenagers – books your child will
grow up with and always remember. So…

FOR THE BEST CHILDREN'S BOOKS,
LOOK FOR THE BEAR